THE DUKE'S YULETIDE BLESSING

A CHRISTMAS REGENCY ROMANCE

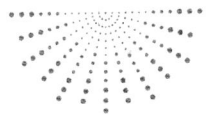

CHARITY MCCOLL

Publisher's Note: This is a work of fiction. Names, characters, places, and incidents are a product of the author's imagination. Locales and public names are sometimes used for atmospheric purposes. Any resemblance to actual people, living or dead, or to businesses, companies, events, institutions, or locales is completely coincidental.

© 2019 PUREREAD LTD

PUREREAD.COM

CONTENTS

1. Locked Away — 1
2. Searching for Hope — 12
3. Don't You Cry, My Queen — 19
4. Homeward Bound — 29
5. In the Spirit of Christmas — 38
6. Dream Me a New Life — 46
7. Unexpected Feelings — 52
8. Winds of Change — 56
9. Exposed Secrets — 62
10. Journey's End — 67
    Epilogue — 70

Our Gift To You — 73

1
LOCKED AWAY

A ndoria Shovia knew that if she was caught, she would be hanged without a trial, or at least a fair one, at that. That was how cruel and vicious their new king was. Anyone who opposed the monarch was immediately termed a traitor and hanged in the public square.

But she was tired of being afraid, and there was a lot at stake here. The future of this beloved kingdom hung in the balance and only one person could ensure that Molorva would one day be free again.

Though she wasn't born in Molorva, it was her mother's homeland, and for the past twenty years this is where she'd lived. Molorva was a small island kingdom just off the coast of Netherlands which had been ruled by monarchs for thousands of years. It was a beautiful and mountainous island which was one of Europe's leading producers of diamonds, sapphires, zircons, agates, and rubies. Because of their wealth, the kingdom was quite developed but also set in their cultural ways, such as owning slaves and bondservants.

Because of a terrible deed done nearly two centuries before, Andoria's mother's family had ended up as bondservants, and only a sitting monarch's Edict of Pardon could overturn that terrible sentence. This meant they had lost all their lands, and apart from small homesteads, they had nothing else. It wasn't an ideal life for Andoria, and she dreamed of one day returning to England where she was born and being free.

Andoria smiled as she slipped through the dark door, careful to make sure none of the guards saw her. The future of Molorva was in the hands of one little baby, and that one as yet unborn, and whose mother was a prisoner in the palace dungeons. A king born in bondage, she thought, shaking her head.

Hearing voices ahead of her, she stopped and pressed her slender body against the wall, heart pounding hard. She hadn't been paying attention and had nearly walked into the guards, which would have ended badly for her. From the voices, she quickly deduced that there were only two of them and she breathed a little easier. Two guards could be dealt with, not a whole legion. But the words of one of them made her blood run cold.

"In just a matter of four months' time, King Francis Kirkon will have no more threats to the kingdom. It has been planned that the day the child of Kaffas is born is the day of his coronation, and that will be around Christmas time. I can't wait for the celebrations then," the guard laughed, a gruff sound that made chills run down Andoria's back. "One full week of doing nothing but celebrating the new king."

"Why does he keep his sister-in-law alive? Why not just kill her and be done with her and the baby?"

"Because Queen Bernice thinks that would be a very easy way out. She hates her half sister and wants her to suffer even more," the two guards laughed. "The deposed queen will first go through the pain of childbirth and then watch as her child is torn from limb to limb on the day of the coronation, an end to Kaffas's lineage. And then she will be given the choice of going into exile or being executed."

"Chilling," the second guard said, "But quite spectacular, not something I would want to miss," and the two men moved out of her hearing range, their laughter fading away.

Andoria's lips tightened. Now more than ever, she needed to get the sweet true queen out of Molorva and take her to safety. It wasn't going to be easy and they might die in the process but there would be no spectacle for those attending the usurper's coronation to see. No, whatever happened, she was going to do her best to get Queen Naomi Kaffas out of those horrible dungeons.

Seeing that the guards had gone in the direction she was headed, Andoria decided to postpone her visit to the dungeons and instead returned to Queen Bernice's chambers and just in time. For the queen walked in a few minutes later and started fussing.

"Andoria, my jewels," Queen Bernice barked at her. "There's a state banquet to discuss our coronation and I want to look my best."

"Yes, your Majesty," Andoria curtsied, her face devoid of any expression. It was an art she had perfected in the past seven years that she had lived and worked in the palace of the country she loved and hated in equal measure.

As the daughter of an Englishman and Molorvan mother, Andoria's features leaned more towards her father's side. Whereas most of the women in Molorva had dark hair and dark skin, Andoria's hair was golden and her eyes blue, and she was the envy of many women. A number of men had expressed the desire to marry her, but she rejected them all, her heart set on one day returning to England to marry an Englishman.

Her father, Ernest Miller, had died when she was two years old and she couldn't even remember him. But her mother had kept his memory alive for her.

"Your father would have been so proud of you," her mother had told her seven years ago when she was chosen to work in the royal palace of Molorva as an apothecary, for she had extensive knowledge in the herbs used in the treatment of various ailments, courtesy of her maternal grandmother. For her own safety, she had also dropped her father's surname and used her mother's instead.

Andoria had also been chosen because she was also one of the few young women in Molorva who spoke perfect English, again because of the extensive lessons she received from her mother.

"Andoria!"

"Your majesty," she curtsied.

"I'll wear my colourless zircons which look like diamonds," Queen Bernice giggled. "It's a game I like to play with his majesty, King Kirkon. When I appear in something other than diamonds before his guests, he will immediately commission the jewellers to make me a set of earrings, bracelet, necklace and rings from real diamonds and gold," she turned her bright eyes to Andoria. "Isn't it wonderful how much my husband really loves me and will do anything for me?"

Andoria wanted to laugh out loud but knew that if she did that, her head would be severed off without mercy.

Queen Bernice was one of the most beautiful women in the kingdom, and songs were written about her, but underneath all that beauty lay a manipulative and vindictive woman. So much ugliness existed within her.

As a servant in the palace and the highest female one at that, Andoria as the queen's lady-in-waiting was revered by the other servants. But she kept her lips shut, so no one would ever misquote her since she held a very enviable position. The reason she was the queen's lady-in-waiting was because of her knowledge of English. Upon ascending to the throne, Queen Bernice had immediately ordered that Andoria be brought from the palace pharmacy to attend to her.

Andoria made it seem like she had very little knowledge of the Molorvan languages of which there were only two. But she was fluent in both dialects, thanks to Grandma Milcah. So, the servants freely gossiped in her presence, believing that she couldn't understand them.

It was through that gossip that Andoria had learned that a number of the young servants had lain with the current king, for he was quite a philanderer. And they received many gifts from him because he was also quite lavish.

King Francis Kirkon was a weak man, according to Andoria, unlike King David Kaffas, the true king of Molorva. Her grandmother used to tell her that a king who was ruled by his base passions of loving power, possessions and women was a weak man and never to be trusted. From when King Kaffas had appointed his cousin to be the Grand Duke of Molorva, her grandmother had predicted disaster for the kingdom just a few weeks before her death.

And her predictions came to pass, for King Francis, who had been the Grand Duke, had murdered his cousin, the king, during a coup five months ago. King Kaffas had been overthrown and murdered and his body buried secretly, according to the rumours running rife in the kingdom. But no one dared speak out loud for fear of being termed a traitor and being executed. Many of the noblemen who had ruled under King Kaffas had gone into exile, and the kingdom was now under the rule of pompous imbeciles, as Grandma Milcah would say, had she still been alive.

Everyone in the kingdom knew that King Kaffas had truly loved his beautiful and sweet wife, who was Queen Bernice's younger half sister. But now wasn't the time to reminisce about the past, and Andoria put her thoughts aside to serve her queen.

"Your majesty, you look so beautiful and adorable, the king won't be able to keep his eyes off you," Andoria had been trained to give the right responses and the queen glowed at the praise.

"More beautiful than my sister?"

Andoria nearly rolled her eyes. It was always the same thing. Bernice had to outshine her sister in every way. She was struggling to get pregnant so her child would be the crown prince or princess but so far, she was unsuccessful. Andoria could have told her that she was wasting her time because, as the person who attended to her in every way, she knew that the queen was barren. But never would such words leave her lips.

"You're the most beautiful jewel in the Kingdom of Molorva," Andoria curtsied. "No matter how beautiful the diamonds, gold and gems of Molorva are, none can hold a shine to my Queen Bernice, fairest of them all."

Helping the queen dress and then walking her to the stateroom where the major domo took over and led her inside was quite taxing, and Andoria was exhausted. Her duties for the next six or so hours were over, and all she had to do was return to the queen's chambers and tidy up after the flurry of dressing activities. But she was also the only one entrusted to take food to the prisoner in the dungeons, and she was the only one who held the keys to the doors leading to the prison. After picking up the lunch dishes from the queen's private dining room, she left the chambers.

As she walked into the kitchen and appreciatively smelled the delicious aromas wafting about in the air, a smile broke out on her face. "Catherine," she called out to the head cook, "You have outdone yourself today, the guests will be very happy. No one can ever do it as well as you, my dear good lady."

"Andoria, you're a gem and I'll spare you a rib or two of wild boar."

"You're the best," Andoria looked around, "I've come to collect the prisoner's food and take it to her."

"In the bin," Catherine pointed her ladle in the direction of the huge bin. "And please stay out of our way because there's so much to do and I don't relish the thought of finding my head on a platter if I should delay even a single dish."

"I'm gone," Andoria went to the other side of the kitchen, away from the hustle and bustle. The large bin contained all the leftover food that even the servants in the palace wouldn't eat. It was put there to feed the palace hogs and dogs and Queen Naomi, as per Queen Bernice's strict instructions.

Using an empty pail, Andoria took as much as she could, glad that the cook and her assistants were too busy to notice that she had picked out the choicest bones. No one knew that Queen Naomi's cute poodle, Silver, lived down in the dungeons with her. The little dog was so faithful to his mistress and kept the dungeon free from rodents and serpents.

Whenever she could, Andoria would take him some choice pieces of meat.

Leaving the pail at the bottom of the stairs, she quickly went to her mistress's chambers and to her side room where she had hidden the food Bernice had left over from lunch. Storing the package under her thick coat, she returned and picked up the pail and walked along the deserted corridor toward the heavy door leading to the dungeon.

"What do you have there," she met the usual guard standing there. His name was Ewan, as he'd told her, and he was mild mannered but she was still very careful around the guards.

"The usurper's dinner," Andoria giggled, sounding like one of the foolish and flirtatious maids. "And I got you something too," she slipped him a small bottle of the best vodka and two pieces of chocolate. "I'll be back as soon as I can." She slipped the key into the lock, turned it and went in, then locked it again.

"You're a beautiful one," she heard him say. "Be back in a jiffy then."

"Very well," she said in a mild tone, but her face was hard. One day, all this would be over.

2

SEARCHING FOR HOPE

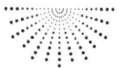

It was hard to think, but he had to. All around him was devastation and all he could do was pray that the weather would be merciful to him and his people this year. Scorching sun for the past two summers followed by extremely harsh winters had caused so much devastation to his duchy. Lord Connor Braxton, Duke of Winthrop, knew that not many people could bear to suffer through more bad weather.

His own fiancée, Lady Serena Marshall, daughter of a lowly baron, had been one of the victims of the terrible weather conditions just two years ago. They had been planning for their wedding and Lady Serena had come to the manor to discuss more about their ceremony which was to have taken place the next year in spring. Even though it was an arranged marriage, Connor had developed a fondness for the fair-haired and blue-eyed woman. She was pretty and vivacious and everyone who knew of their engagement had agreed that she would make a good wife to him and a suitable duchess and would beget strong and healthy sons.

Much as Connor yearned for some passion in their relationship, he knew that Serena with her uptight upbringing wasn't going to provide it. So, he had resigned himself to having a comfortable marriage in the days to come, but that wasn't to be.

On that fateful day, Serena had visited him and halfway through the visit, it started snowing. She announced that she had to go back home even though the manor had many empty rooms that she could have used.

"Please stay," he begged. "When it stops snowing, I'll take you home in my carriage, no matter what time it is."

Serena shook her head, "I rode over and besides, what's a little snow? I've ridden in blizzards, and my home is only a mile down the road from here," she said.

"The weather isn't good and I don't like you being out there on your own. Or at least let me get my horse saddled and I'll come with you."

"Don't be such a fussy mother hen," she brushed his protestations aside and picked up her crop and jumped onto her horse. She waved as she left, and it was with a heavy heart that he'd watched her go.

As he was getting ready for bed that evening, his valet walked into his bedchamber or more like burst in, his face very white. It wasn't like Rupert to behave in such a manner and Connor frowned. "What's going on, Rupert?"

"Your Grace," the man looked shaken. *"I'm afraid I have very bad news."*

"What is it?"

"Lady Serena met with an accident when she left here and has been taken to her father's house, but the doctor says she may not last the night."

But Serena had lived in a vegetative state for a full year, during which every physician and surgeon had done what they could for her but all in vain. Connor hadn't spared any money to make sure that his fiancée was treated, and when his own ran out, he turned to borrowing from whoever could lend him. In the end, just a year ago, Serena had succumbed to her injuries. While she still lived, Connor's creditors had stayed at bay, but after her death, they had hounded him mercilessly.

The Winthrop Duchy, a once-prosperous and successful entity had suffered terrible summers and winters, and his tenants were unable to meet their obligations to him, which further put him in a lot of debt. He dug into his coffers and, in the end, it was like chasing after the wind.

For a full year, he'd been struggling to pay off what he owed but was still a long way from being free. While a few peers whose help he sought advised him to sell part of his estate and recover, he knew that he could never do it.

He'd made a promise to his grandfather that he would keep the estate intact, and he intended to keep his promise even though things were really tough now.

Autumn was nigh, and he could hear the wind whistling in the trees. The windows rattled as they kept the fierce winds at bay.

"What am I going to do?" He asked himself as he went to check on his horses. They were the only precious assets he still had, and come the New Year, he was going to have to sell at least two of them to pacify the creditors. He had five prize horses that he knew would fetch him a tidy sum, but that was a drop in the ocean in as far as his debts went. He would need to do more to get himself out of this problem.

The five Arabian horses were in their stalls, and Caleb, his stableman, was pouring oats into their troughs. They all knew him and came closer as he patted each of them in turn.

"Caleb, the wind is getting very strong. Do you think the horses are in any danger?"

"Your grace," the man effected the perfect bow. "I reinforced the walls, but we should pray for mild winds this year."

"And your own quarters?" Caleb lived above the stable. When he'd come to work on the estate about four months ago, the rooms were nothing but bare space, since the other workers all had cottages. Sadly, they had all left to find employment on other estates when it because obvious that the Winthrop Duchy could no longer sustain their wages.

Caleb had turned the empty room into comfortable quarters for himself, and not for the first time, Connor wondered who the strong and silent man was.

Caleb had a way with the horses and never once had Connor found him drunk or disorderly. He was the perfect gentleman and for him to be a stableman made the duke wonder if perhaps he had been born into a family of means but had fallen on hard times.

They were of the same height and build, but whereas Connor's hair was fair, Caleb's was dark. Connor had asked him where he'd learned how to take such good care of horses and with a smile, Caleb had told him that he'd worked for a travelling circus from Europe. Connor believed him for he'd heard the man speaking a foreign language to the animals. The dialect sounded much like that spoken by the gypsies who from time came to the estate.

"My quarters are safe, thank you for your concern, Your Grace."

"You need to be safe, Caleb," Connor looked around the stable noting that as always, the place was very clean. "If there's anything you need at all, just come to the house and get it."

"Much obliged, Your Grace."

Connor nodded and left the stables, walking back into the house through the cold kitchen. His once-warm kitchen was now deserted and it was only

Rupert of all his older servants, who had refused to leave.

"You gave me the best when the duchy was prospering," the man had told the duke when he asked if he should give him a reference to get a position with another nobleman. *"Why should I abandon you in your hour of need, Your Grace?"* And so, the man had stayed.

Rupert's wife, Emily, came by once a day to prepare a meal for the duke, which lasted until the next day. Connor insisted that Caleb takes all meals with him and the two men would often sit in the dining room and talk about many things. It amazed Connor that Caleb was so knowledgeable about a variety of topics, and their dinners were never quiet ones. He liked the man and wished he could do more for him but even he was struggling.

3

DON'T YOU CRY, MY QUEEN

Andoria looked down at the sleeping queen. The woman had less than one week to deliver her child and after that, both their fates would be sealed. She shook her head slowly and vowed that it would not happen, not while she was still alive.

She'd come in earlier and taken the little dog for a romp further down into the dungeons and it was Silver who had showed her the way out of this place.

Kneeling down beside the queen, she gently shook her awake, "My Queen, it's time to leave."

"Are you sure about this, Andoria?"

"I'm not sure about anything but if we don't leave today, it may be too late. Today is our last chance to get out of here because the last trawler going to England leaves the docks in six hours' time. They won't be back until after Christmas and by then," Andoria shrugged.

"Save yourself, Andoria," Queen Naomi took her hand and gave her a sad smile. "I've made peace with whatever will come. It looks like this is where it will all end."

"Your Royal Highness, the throne of Molorva, which you swore to protect on the day you married King Kaffas, lies in your hands. This baby is the future king or queen, the hope of all Molorvans. I know that while many might betray you, many more are praying for you and this child. You owe them that much, my Queen."

"But if we're caught, you'll be beheaded and I'll be brought back here to await my terrible fate after I deliver my child," the queen sighed. "I love my sister so much, but she has never accepted me, just like she never accepted my mother after our father married her. It wasn't my mother's fault that Papa put Bernice's mother away, but it was because of her infidelities which were so common and done openly." Naomi shook her head, "Did you know that Bernice was betrothed to King Kaffas from when they were children, but after her mother's shameful deeds, that honour was withdrawn and bestowed upon me. My sister has never forgiven me for falling in love with David and he with me."

"They say that destiny may be derailed and delayed but it can never be denied, my Queen. Now, why don't we make sure that the throne of Molorva is preserved?"

"Will it really matter if we're caught, Andoria? We could all die for nothing in the end."

"But if we're not caught, we will make it back to my Fatherland, where you will be safe, and I know the world will never let another tyrant like Napoleon live and rule in his wickedness. It's a well-known fact that Francis Kirkon is extremely ambitious, and with a manipulative queen by his side, who's to say they won't try to make themselves conquerors of the world? You have the backing of powerful countries, the countries which formed that Coalition Forces that took Napoleon on and defeated him, and now he's now banished to St. Helena forever."

Naomi twisted her lips, "Why didn't they come to our aid when it mattered five months ago," her eyes filled with tears. "When my husband's cousin overthrew the king, why didn't they come forth and help then?"

"My Queen, you have to remember that at the time they were dealing with Napoleon after he escaped from Elba. But now things have settled down, and I know they will help you. The only way they can help is if they know that you're still alive and this child comes into the world. Right now, the rumour is that after King Kaffas died, you didn't live long after that. According to many out there, your husband's lineage ended. You're the hope of the Molorvans, my Queen. Please do not give up now when we're so close to the finish line."

The queen was silent for a while and Andoria forced herself not to panic because time was running out for them. But finally, Naomi raised her head and nodded.

"Let's do this then but one thing puzzles me. Andoria, how did you manage to make sure that we won't be followed?"

Andoria smiled, retaining her secret for the moment. "I have my ways, my Queen. But we have to move now. You'll be glad to know that Silver is the one who found a way out and I have prepared the baskets."

"Baskets? What for?" Naomi struggled to her feet and allowed Andoria to put a smelly cloak around her. "This thing stinks and I might be sick all over it."

"Please take deep breaths for this is part of our disguise that will help us get out of this palace."

"What do you mean, Andoria?"

"You'll see," Andoria stepped aside and observed the queen. "No one will recognize you," she smeared some tar on the queen's face to make her countenance darker and did the same for herself.

"You're very brave," Naomi chuckled softly, "Foolish but brave."

"I'm a revolutionary to the last drop of blood in my body, my Queen. Now, shall we go?"

"What's in that heavy bag you're carrying?"

"Just some things that we'll need on our journey and food that I stole from the kitchen for us to eat since we have five days before we get to England."

"You think of everything and I'm just sorry that I never realised your worth when I was queen," Naomi said sadly. "But one day, I will find a way of rewarding you for what you're doing for me."

Slipping out of the palace through the secret passageway wasn't all that difficult. She wrapped the little dog in dirty rugs. "Silver, you must not make a single sound," and the dog gave a small bark to show that he understood. She put him in her own fish basket together with the canvas bag. There were still obstacles they would face along the way but Andoria believed that they were under the Lord's protection during this Christmas season.

They silently walked towards the large palace gates, meeting people coming and going, and they fell in with them. Many villagers usually brought their produce to the palace at all hours of the day and night. The guards didn't find it strange to see two dirty-looking women carrying baskets made from reeds on their heads.

"If you take a good wash, I might be tempted to be attracted to you," one of the guards turned his nose up at the heavy fish smell emanating from Naomi and Andoria's baskets. "Get your stinking selves out of here before I whip you soundly," he growled at them.

"Pardon, Sir," she slipped him a gold guinea, "Thank you for your help," she laid on a thick accent. "We'll be going now," the man didn't bother with them, waving them away as he pocketed the guinea.

Once they were out of the gates, Andoria sighed with relief. "This is all gratitude to your husband, my Queen. He made it possible for this to happen. Thank God for his rule that no villager bringing their produce should ever be turned away from the palace whether day or night."

Naomi just smiled sadly in the darkness. She missed David, and even though she knew that she would never see him again, the baby she carried in her womb would be the way she remembered him.

Andoria knew that the queen was thinking about her handsome husband. King David Kaffas was one of the few men Andoria respected, honoured, admired and would willingly die for. That was the reason she'd taken this mission upon herself, without telling a single soul.

Upon ascending to the throne four years ago, he'd shut down all his father's harems in the capital city, Longria, and in his country palace in Boloise, both now taken over by his cousin. King Kaffas had granted all the concubines their freedom. What's more, he gave each of them a large dowry, and many of them had eventually found good men to marry them, men who could bear their shame and love them still.

Under his rule, Molorva's economy had grown in leaps and bounds and though his soldiers hadn't been part of the Coalition Forces fighting Napoleon because he felt they weren't properly trained, he had provided vast resources from finances to timber to build battleships, which were greatly appreciated. That was why Andoria was sure that once the Allies found out that Queen Naomi was alive and had borne a child for the dead king, they would step in and restore the throne to the Kaffas Lineage.

It was actually during a visit to Prussia to meet with the Allies that his cousin, King Francis Kirkon had deposed him in a bloodless coup, calling him a sell-out to the foreign legions because the latter supported Napoleon. At the time, many people had rallied behind the charismatic King Francis, but it wasn't long before they realized the grave mistake they had made. The man was a maniac and tyrant, and the people of Molorva discovered that when it was too late and their beloved king was dead, believed to have been assassinated by his cousin.

Half a mile down the road, they discarded the heavy baskets and smelly clothes and Andoria picked Silver up. They had only gone a few steps when Andoria thought she heard someone following them. Since she had taken a path that wasn't used much, she was sure that whoever was coming up behind them didn't have good intentions. She pulled Naomi into a dark alley.

"What?"

"Sh!" Andoria placed a hand over the queen's lips and prayed that Silver wouldn't growl and not too soon. Two sets of footsteps hurried past them.

"You're sure you saw the two women coming this way?" One gruff voice said.

"Yes, just follow the fishy smell. They have money and I know this because they were paid a good sum at the palace for their fish. And also, I don't mind enjoying their favours."

Andoria was glad they had rid themselves of the smelly baskets and garments or else the vagabonds might have found their hiding spot. And Silver behaved himself by remaining completely silent. She waited until the men's voices faded away into the distance before moving.

"We have to use the side roads," she tucked the dog in one hand and the heavy bag she carried in the other. "It will take slightly longer but it's much safer."

"Just go on without me," Naomi breathed heavily.

"Your Majesty, we have twelve hours before the drugs I administered to the queen and guards wear off and people come after us. By that time, we'll be in England. Please do not give up now, victory is so close at hand."

"Let's go," Naomi's voice was stronger, and Andoria smiled in the darkness. Yes, they would get to safety.

It took them nearly two hours to get to the docks, but they met no further obstacles on the way. Just as they rounded the final turn to the docks, the large trawler's horn tooted, a sign that it would be leaving shortly.

"Just in time," Andoria said, taking Naomi's hand and they hurried up the gangway.

4

HOMEWARD BOUND

The harsh retching woke her up and Andoria knew that the queen was sick again. Poor woman had hardly been able to keep anything down for the five days they'd been on the sea. But in just a few hours' time, the trawler would dock in London, and they would be free.

"Your Majesty, I'm sorry about all this."

"Andoria," Naomi wiped her face. It was morning, and light poured into the small space they had been put in. "It's just motion sickness, but I'll be all right."

"We'll soon be in London, and you can get better food than stale bread and cheese."

Naomi smiled, "Beggars can't be choosers, and we're better than those who have nothing to eat." She looked around the room. "What do you think this trawler carries?"

"Usually it's timber from Molorva, which is taken to London, and on the way back they carry luxury items for Queen Bernice. That's how I found out that this was the best way for us to get out of London. Luckily, only the skipper knows that I work for the queen, and he's a strong supporter of your husband, else he wouldn't have allowed us to come aboard."

"Can he be trusted?"

"With the last breath of his life, my Queen. But I don't know about the other sailors."

"I long for a glass of refreshing melon juice, like the one you used to sneak to me in the dungeons."

"When we get to where we're going, I'll make sure you get plenty of melon juice. In the meantime, I'll go and get you some fresh water," Andoria looked at the coloured substance in the bottle that they had drunk in their days of confinement and knew that she couldn't take any more.

Naomi shook her head, "You know what the Skipper said, that we should keep out of sight and out of trouble. We don't need to court any trouble now."

"My Queen, we're just a few hours from docking, I don't think we have to worry about anything."

"Andoria, just be careful out there."

"I promise to be careful," she slipped out of the small cabin. It was actually a storage room next to the Skipper's quarters. She had parted with a substantial amount of money and two topaz stones, but it was all worth it. Thanks to Queen Bernice's vanity and greed, there was usually a lot of money in her chambers and jewels too. In the five days they'd been on the ship, no one had bothered them and Andoria knew it was because of the kindly skipper. But he had been clear that they should stay out of sight on the all-male boat.

Andoria didn't want to get into trouble but the queen needed water because she was very weak. She hadn't been able to contain any food. The moment Andoria stepped onto deck, she realised that she had made a terrible mistake. One of the sailors spotted her and she retreated, heart pounding but he followed, telling his colleagues that he was going to relieve himself.

"Now, what is a beautiful woman doing on this rig, and where have you been hiding yourself?" Even though he spoke English, Andoria recognized him to be Molorvan.

"Sir, I don't want any trouble," she was terrified at the wicked gleam she saw in his eyes. Why hadn't she listened to Naomi and stayed in their room? She didn't want him to find out that the queen was on the ship, for she had no idea where his loyalties lay. Once they were safely in England then they could walk around freely, but not yet.

"Well, Little Lady," he drew closer and she could smell the whiskey on his breath. She retreated until her back was against the door of their small cabin and she hoped Naomi would hear them talking and hide herself under the sacks or in a barrel. "I believe this is a storage room and will be quite ideal for what I have in mind for us," the sailor said. "Open it and get in," he looked around to see if anyone was coming but the corridors were empty. "Better that you have only me to deal with than ten or fifteen more of my colleagues."

"Yes, sir," she pretended to accept his terms and entered the room, which she saw was empty, and panicked at first. Then she noticed the queen crouching behind the door, and she moved farther in, drawing the unsuspecting man inside. Then

Naomi moved swiftly and struck a blow to the back of his head. He crumpled to the floor with a grunt.

"Quick," Naomi ordered a stunned Andoria. "Drag him inside and lock the door," she ordered. "Let's bind him securely and pray that no one comes to look for us while he's here. Let them find him when we're off the ship. Silver, find me some rope," she told the dog then snapped her fingers at Andoria. "Focus and help Silver find rope."

"Yes, of course," Andoria couldn't believe that the genteel queen who had looked so helpless could pack such a punch and was now standing over the unconscious man, staring down at him. Her features had changed, and she looked ready for battle.

"Andoria, you made me have hope again," Naomi said placing a hand over her swollen belly. "This is the future ruler of Molorva, and I'm going to protect this child with my last breath."

"Yes, Your Majesty."

"Now, bind this man up and let's pray that he doesn't recover consciousness before we dock and get out of here."

The Duchy of Winthrop and its village lay about fifty miles northwest of London, and Andoria quickly found them a coach headed in that direction. She was glad they were finally in England, and no one spared them a second glance. They looked like ordinary women headed north for Christmas.

But a new problem had presented itself. It was the day before Christmas Eve, and she knew the Queen's time was very near. She seemed to be having contractions which she was trying very hard to hide. It had also started snowing heavily and the coach driver was already talking of abandoning the whole journey if the snow didn't stop falling in the next few hours.

"Please Sir," Andoria begged. "I have to get my sister home before she delivers her baby."

The chubby man shrugged, "Can't control the weather, Miss. I have to take care of myself and other passengers too. Why not get a room in one of the inns around and wait out the snow?"

Andoria shook her head, "It's important that we get home before Christmas, Sir. Please."

"Well, I can't promise anything, but you better pray that the snow stops or else even if we begin the journey, we may have to stop at one of the inns along the way. Tomorrow is Christmas Eve, and much as I want to rush and be back to London to be with my family, I may have to postpone the whole journey altogether."

But the weather favoured the journey, and they were soon on their way. Silver lay nestled on Naomi's lap and seemed to be keeping her calm, even though Andoria could see that the journey was taking its toll. The coach driver promised that they would be in Winthrop in eight hours.

There were two men who spoke in low tones, and from the clothes they wore, Andoria guessed that they were clerks probably going home for the holidays. Then there was a young couple, and from the shy looks they kept giving each other and the shiny rings on their fingers, they were obviously newlyweds. They were lost in their own world, and Andoria felt a pang in her heart. These two were so much in love, and they reminded her of King David and Queen Naomi and the love they had shared. As well, there was a woman with two children and a third on the way. She and Naomi chatted about their experiences but Andoria chose to stare at the passing scenery. This was home, her fatherland and she was finally here. Her journey had led her to this place, and she wondered how it would all end.

Andoria had no idea what she was going to tell the duke when they showed up at his door. All she knew about him was what her mother had told her, which wasn't really much, given that Georgia Shovia had only lived in Winthrop Village for three years. But according to her parent, the old duke was very kind and cared about all those who lived on his estate and Winthrop village. One way or another, she was going to convince the duke to help them, especially the queen. Then she would search for any of her father's remaining relatives, though she didn't hold onto much hope. At the time her mother had decided to return to Molorva twenty years ago, all the family had been wiped out because of a measles outbreak and the two of them were lucky to have survived it.

"This is your stop, young ladies," the coachman said, pulling into the courtyard of a small inn. "Good luck with getting to your final destination in this weather."

"Would you take us up to the Duke's manor?" Andoria was hoping against all hope.

The man shook his head, "This is as far as I can take you, because as you can see, I still have other passengers to convey a further twenty miles from here. But don't worry, it's just a mile down the road," he pointed at a path.

He let them down at the Stoke's Inn and the coach left shortly after. Andoria looked at the queen with compassion.

"Why don't you stay here, my Queen, and I'll go to the manor and ask for a cart to come and bring you there."

But Naomi firmly shook her head, "We've come this far, and the man said we only have a mile to go. Nothing can stop me now."

"But . . ."

"Andoria, I'll not have you arguing with me. Let Silver walk ahead of us and I will lean on you."

"Yes, My Queen."

5

IN THE SPIRIT OF CHRISTMAS

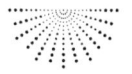

He was going to spend Christmas alone this year, and the thought filled him with much dread. Last Christmas, people who had come to help him bury Serena had filled the house, but that wasn't the case this year. Everyone was gone, and he was sure Caleb would be leaving the next day to go and be with his family.

"I hate this loneliness," he murmured as he lit the fire in the living room grate. This house had been built to have many people and children in it, and he remembered all the Christmases when he'd been young and his grandparents were still alive. The house would be filled with laughter and the sound of music from flutes and harps. All that had ended five years ago when his grandfather died and his grandmother followed shortly. Even though he'd celebrated Christmas after that, it had been on a much quieter scale.

He thought of asking Caleb to stay with him, but that would be selfish. Everyone needed to be with their families at this time and he'd even told Rupert not to report to work until the New Year.

"Oh Lord," he prayed, "If only someone—anyone—would come and celebrate this holiday with me, it would really cheer me up. Christmas should be spent with family, but I have none," he sank despondently onto the couch in front of the fire, gazing broodingly at the fire.

Emily had made him a large pie which he was sure would last him until Christmas Day, if he ate frugally. Then an idea popped into his head. He needed to get out of the house or else his dismal thoughts would drive him out of his mind.

It had stopped snowing and even though it was late afternoon, there was some sunshine, and he decided to go hunting. Some wild meat would look good on his table over Christmas. As he stepped into the stable, he was surprised to find Caleb feeding the horses.

"Caleb," he looked at the stableman, "I expected you to have left by now, or have you decided that you will leave tomorrow morning? You need to be with your family over Christmas. Tomorrow is Christmas Eve, and your family must be expecting you."

"Yes, Your Grace, I was just finishing up with the feeding and watering of the animals; then I'll be gone," he looked around the stable. "Who will take care of the horses while I'm away?"

"I'll do it so you can have time with your family. If you like, you can return in the New Year," Connor reached into his pocket. "I don't have much, but this sovereign should buy you something to bring to your family. Maybe some candy for your little ones."

"Thank you very much," Caleb bowed.

"Or maybe you can leave tomorrow morning," Connor said, and Caleb looked at him questioningly. He gave a brief laugh, "Perhaps I could impose on your company for a few more hours."

"Whatever you need, my lord."

"At this time of year, my woods are teeming with wild hogs. Perhaps we shall be lucky to catch a sizeable one; then you can have something more to take to your family tomorrow."

"I'd like that very much," the man said in his usual quiet voice.

The woods were not only teeming with wild hogs but rabbits and pheasants as well, and villagers who started when the duke came upon them. "No, go ahead and hunt for as much game as can feed your families over Christmas but don't be wasteful," he told them, and they shuffled off.

The two men returned home nearly two hours later with a large hog and broad smiles on their faces. The meat would serve them for a number of days.

"I didn't realise that my woods are so well populated with game," Connor remarked, as they dressed the hog together and put it over the blazing fire in the kitchen. Soon there was a delicious aroma, and the duke couldn't help but lick his lips with anticipation of what was to come. They both feasted well, and Caleb left after that. Connor assumed that he was going to bed early so he could prepare for his journey home.

When Connor was replete, he took his place in front of the still blazing fire in the living room and had began dozing with he heard a knock at the front door. Since there was no one else in the manor to open the door, he groaned as he got to his feet and shuffled barefooted and opened the door. Dusk was fast falling and snow with it, and he was surprised at what he saw.

It was the most beautiful woman he'd ever set his eyes on, and his heart began racing. "I must be seeing an apparition," he looked over her shoulder to see if there was a carriage waiting but the road was empty behind them and far beyond. He wasn't aware that he'd said the words out loud until he saw the young woman smile. And a small dog barked at her feet then slipped into the house.

⁓

"My Queen, you should have waited at the inn," Andoria said when they'd been walking for about an hour. Silver would run ahead yapping at small rodents in the undergrowth but caught nothing, then would return panting and wagging his little tail. He kept them entertained but Andoria wished they would get to their destination. The queen was really tired.

"Andoria, you know how impatient I get when someone keeps repeating themselves," but her sweet smile took the sting out of her words. "I see a gate up ahead which means that we shall shortly be coming up to a house."

"You're right," Andoria was excited. She felt the heavy burden on her shoulders. If something happened to the queen or her unborn child, Molorva would never forgive her, and the wicked tyrants sitting unlawfully on the throne would have won without lifting a finger. The future of that country lay in her hands, and she prayed for strength for both of them.

There was a large house ahead and she picked the dog up, not wanting him to rush into trouble. Andoria wished she could pick Naomi up and carry her for the rest of the way since it had started snowing.

But finally, they were at the door and she placed the dog on the ground. A most delicious aroma assailed her nostrils, causing her stomach to growl in response.

"Wait," Naomi held her hand as she raised it to knock on the door.

"What is it, my Queen?"

"We don't know what lies on the other side of this door, but I want you to promise me one thing."

"Anything you want, your Majesty."

"If anything happens to me, please keep this child safe. I know that the people of Molorva will one day come for him or her, so please do not let anything bad happen to this child."

"I promise," Andoria saw how weary her mistress was. "Please allow me to knock so we can get you a place to rest."

"Go ahead," Naomi leaned tiredly against the side of the door but was out of sight.

Andoria raised her hand and knocked and a few minutes later, she heard footsteps walking up to the door. The man who opened the door took her breath away.

She had seen a number of handsome men in Molorva but this one stunned her. Even though he was an Englishman with fair hair and blue eyes, his dark skin told of a man who spent a lot of time in the outdoors.

"I must be seeing an apparition," the way he spoke in a cultured voice told her that this was probably a servant of high ranking, or maybe the duke's son.

She smiled him, "I assure you that we're real," she said, then laughed. "Silver, come back here," she called out to the dog which had disappeared into the house. "I'm sorry, but we're so weary."

"You and the dog?"

Andoria shook her head and pointed at Queen Naomi. "This is my mistress and she's due to have her baby at any time."

6

DREAM ME A NEW LIFE

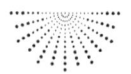

The queen was fed and fast asleep in the duchess's beautiful suite. Andoria knew the man downstairs was waiting for answers, which she was now ready to provide.

The moment he'd caught sight of Naomi, he had carried her into the house in his strong arms and then placed her on the couch before the fire. "You're cold but thank goodness there's a fire. And you look hungry too."

Without asking any questions, he provided them with a nice meal of roast potatoes and ham and then showed them to this beautiful room after they were done eating. Andoria had protested but he smiled at her.

"This is the best room in the house and the only one which doesn't need a fire lit in it. It belonged to my mother and was built to withstand the cold, because Mama was very frail, and smoke from the fire affected her," he said. "Besides, the maid's room next door is also warm enough, and the two of you should be very comfortable."

That was when she realised that this was the Duke of Winthrop, and a very young and handsome one too.

He had showed her where to fetch water and heated it. "My stableman has gone to be with his family or else he would have helped you," he'd said, but she didn't mind. This felt like home and after giving her mistress her bath, she had dressed her in the warm clothes the duke had provided from one of his mother's trunks.

What's more, he showed her the closet where rows and rows of beautiful gowns hung. "Feel free to use any of them, for they have been unused for nearly two decades."

After her bath and when she was sure Naomi was asleep, she chose a simple emerald silky gown and a shawl then combed her hair and left it flowing, then went downstairs.

Connor rose to his feet as soon as she walked into the living room and she knew he had been listening for her. "Would you like a glass of spiced hot port?" he asked. "I use honey and lemons to make it very mild, but it's good for the cold." He couldn't believe that this beautiful woman was in his house and so close. So, this was the passion that people sang about and which men had killed for. So strong were his feelings for this stranger that he thought he must be going mad.

"You're so kind," Andoria said, waiting to be invited to sit.

"Please sit in front of the fire so you'll be warm," he said. He couldn't believe that his prayers had been answered, and he wouldn't be alone over Christmas. Whatever happened, he was going to make sure that his two beautiful guests stayed for as long as possible. He poured out a generous amount of the spiced port and then handed the glass to her. "And tell me everything and why you would risk a pregnant woman's life and drag her into the cold."

Silver was dozing in front of the fire and he flicked his tail lazily just to make them aware that he was present. Like them, the little dog had enjoyed a delicious meal, licking his plate clean.

"Yes, Sir," she took a sip of the drink and found that she quite liked the mild taste. Like he'd said, the honey and lemons masked the alcohol taste. "The woman asleep upstairs is Queen Naomi Kaffas, the wife of King David Kaffas of Molorva Kingdom in Northern Europe." Andoria smiled at the stunned look on the duke's face. "I gather from your expression that you've heard of the royal family of Molorva."

Connor nodded, "I've heard about the Kingdom of Molorva and the coup that took place five or six months ago and that the king was assassinated. But I'm not a politician and steer clear of anything to do with politics so I don't know much else. But how is it that the queen sleeps upstairs and you're here?"

Andoria told him everything that had happened and also about their journey, pausing from time to time to sip from her glass. She felt warm and quite lazy, but she couldn't sleep until she had finished her story.

"Andoria is putting it all very mildly," Naomi's voice floated to her from the doorway and she quickly shot to her feet.

"My Queen, I thought you were asleep."

"Well, I caught a brief nap but this little one," she held her stomach with both hands. "Won't give me any peace; it's as though this child wants to come into the world as soon as possible."

"Are you in pain?" Andoria helped her to the couch and then put her feet up on a small footstool.

"Andoria, would you stop fussing and sit down?" Naomi smiled and turned to the duke who was watching them silently. "This young woman is quite exceptional. In all the time that I was a prisoner in the palace dungeons, she kept me alive and well fed. They would send her with food fit for pigs and dogs but somehow, I ended up eating steak and chicken instead. I don't know how she did it but," Naomi chuckled, "Andoria and the dog kept me alive and hopeful even when I would have given up. She risked her life so many times to keep me and the future ruler of Molorva alive," her features fell, and Connor saw the deep sadness in her eyes. "My husband was taken away and assassinated but they didn't even bring me back his body so I could bury him," her voice caught on a sob. "I lost hope, but Andoria wouldn't let me quit. She refused to let me give up, and here we are now. What makes me sad is that my husband never lived to see the birth of his first child."

"Your Majesty," the duke's voice was soft and full of compassion. "I'm very sorry for your loss, and I'll do everything I can to ensure that you and the future ruler of Molorva are safe and remain so until he or she can assume the throne of King Kaffas. You're welcome to live in my home for as long as you need to."

"We thank you for being so kind, and one day, the people of Molorva will reward you for your noble service to their queen and crown prince or princess." Naomi yawned. "I'm so tired but unable to sleep."

"Before he left, Caleb made some hot chocolate. Miss Andoria, why don't you fetch some for the queen."

"Yes, Your Grace," and she hurried to do as bid.

Naomi looked at the duke, "Caleb? Who's that?"

"He's my stableman. The man came to me nearly six months ago, or rather I found him lying unconscious under my hedge. He looked like he'd been attacked by some people and I brought him here and when he was well, asked to be my stableman. Seeing as tomorrow is Christmas Eve, I believe he's gone to be with his family. I pray that he gets there before the snow makes it impossible for him to travel."

7

UNEXPECTED FEELINGS

"I feel like I want to throw up," Naomi said, her chest heaving. Andoria could see that she was in a lot of pain but was trying not to cry out.

Back in Molorva, Andoria had assisted her grandmother deliver many babies and she knew just what to do. But this was no ordinary citizen of Molorva or baby that she was about to deliver, it was the next ruler of the kingdom.

"Here is a water basin," Andoria held it closer and Naomi emptied whatever little was left in her stomach.

"I just wish this baby would come out and let me rest," the queen leaned back weakly against the pillows, a hand to her forehead. She was sweating and Andoria wiped her face. "David had promised that he would be here with me," she started crying, dry sobs with no tears. "He left me, left us all alone."

"My Queen, please calm down."

"My husband didn't deserve to be assassinated like a traitor. David was a good man and an honourable king. He gave himself to Molorva, but they turned on him and instead embraced that wicked man. They don't deserve my baby."

Andoria knew that it was the pain talking and she let the woman rant on. Getting it all out of her system would help keep her mind off the difficult task of delivery that lay ahead.

"I should hold onto my baby and not let those ingrates have him or her," her words ended on a loud moan. She screamed and wriggled on the bed. "It hurts so much."

There was a gush of water and Andoria sighed with relief. It was nearly time for the king or queen of Molorva to be born, and she was ready. "My Queen, it's nearly time and I'm ready."

After a few more puffs and pants, Naomi brought forth a son, a healthy boy who gave a lusty cry, and the two women laughed.

"He's so beautiful and will grow up to be as handsome as his father was," Andoria cut the cord that bound mother and child and placed him on Naomi's chest. The queen was laughing and crying at the same time.

"Welcome to the world," Andoria gave a deep curtsey in reverence to the new-born king. "Hail the King of Molorva."

"His name is Noel Kaffas," his mother said, kissing him all over his face, uncaring that he wasn't yet cleaned up.

"Hail King Noel Kaffas, ruler of Molorva Kingdom," and once again, Andoria curtsied. "How blessed am I to see the birth of this great man."

She cleaned up the baby and his mother and when they were comfortable, she took care of the room.

∼

Connor was glad that the screaming had stopped. He'd never heard a woman delivering a baby before and it gave him new respect for all mothers. Never again would he disrespect a woman, and he made a promise to himself that when he finally got married, he would always treat his wife with kindness and respect. It was only befitting given that she would have to go through much pain to bring their children into the world.

He heard a step and looked up, "Your Grace," Andoria curtsied, "Queen Naomi says you can come and meet the new-born king."

"And I'm greatly honoured," he said a short while later when he was standing in the duchess's chambers. He bowed to the mother and child. "Hail the King of Molorva."

"His name is King Noel Kaffas," Andoria said.

"I salute you, O King Noel of Kaffas. May your reign be long and prosperous, and may you bring light and hope to your people."

"May your words be prophecy indeed," Andoria said, and they both bowed to mother and child.

8
WINDS OF CHANGE

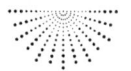

There was a soft footfall on the landing and the three of them looked toward the door, quite puzzled as to who it could be. The moment the man appeared in the doorway, Naomi and Andoria screamed, startling the sleeping child who let out a wail of his own.

Connor straightened up, ready to defend the two women. "Caleb, what's the meaning of all this? You've frightened the women." Connor demanded of his stableman who merely smiled, never once taking his eyes off Naomi and the baby whose cries had hushed down.

"Your Majesty," Andoria gave a deep curtsey and Connor stared at her in confusion.

"My love," Naomi whispered from the bed.

"Your Grace," Andoria turned to Connor, "May I present to you, King David Kaffas, ruler of Molorva Kingdom."

"What!" Connor was stunned. "King David Kaffas of Molorva? But everyone thought you'd been assassinated."

"And that worked in my favour," the king said. "May I be allowed to come in and greet my queen and new-born son?"

"Of course, of course," Connor said. "How is it that you ended up in my stables working for me?"

"It's a long story, which I'll share once my hands have held my loved ones."

Connor nodded and Andoria curtsied once more; then they both left the room.

"This is a miracle," Andoria led the way to the living room and sat down in front of the fire. "Silver, our king is alive and well."

"This is such a fantastic event that I believe I'm dreaming."

King Kaffas came down to the living room after nearly two hours. "I can't thank you enough, Andoria. You saved and preserved the Kingdom of Molorva and my beautiful queen. How will I ever reward you?"

"It was my pleasure serving you, my King."

"The queen and prince are asleep."

"Caleb, er . . . Your Majesty, please forgive me for putting you to work in the stables."

"You couldn't have known who I was when you found me lying under your hedge. And you saved my life because no one would expect a king to work in the stables. The thing is, I have no idea how I got to this part of England. After the coup, I was arrested and taken to the dungeons in Boloise, my country seat, but there, I still had many loyal followers. They sneaked me out of the palace and put me on a boat to England. I was supposed to go to the Duke of Worchestershire because he is a good friend of my uncle. My queen and I had visited him once and I knew that I would be safe with him. But someone must have followed me for the next thing I knew, I was attacked and robbed of all that I had. Then I woke up here in this house."

"No one could tell where you came from when I tried to find out after finding you lying under the hedge, but that's not important. We're just happy that you're alive. What do you intend to do?"

"I've been communicating with the current Grand Duke of Molorva."

"Lord Richard?" Andoria asked.

"Yes. He's one of the good ones left in the kingdom, and even though he's Francis's father, he is loyal to me. You see, Francis is his son by one of his concubines and was brought home when he was about ten years old. Francis has always been a rebel, and much as his father tried to keep him on the straight path, he chose his own way."

"What will happen to him now?"

"The law of Molorva is clear on how traitors are to be treated. He'll be given the option of exile or execution. Knowing my cousin, he'll choose exile because he thinks that he will be like Napoleon and escape from where he'll be taken," the king chuckled, "He has no idea what exile for a Molorvan means."

The monarch looked really fierce and Andoria didn't envy his enemies.

They were having a late simple breakfast prepared by Andoria, and the two men insisted that she join them at the table when she cocked her head to one side, "Do you hear that?"

"Yes," Connor walked to the window. "I see a number of carriages coming up the driveway and have no idea who could be visiting today of all days. It's Christmas Day, and most people are at home celebrating the holidays with their families."

Andoria joined him at the window, "From what I can see, those are mighty fine carriages, probably your noble friends coming to visit you."

He shook his head with a small laugh, "I doubt it, but shall we find out who it is?"

It was the king's maternal uncle, and another man Andoria recognized. She curtsied just as King Kaffas joined them at the doorway.

"My uncle," King Kaffas touched the older man's feet. "I greet you, O Grand Duke of Molorva."

"Hail to the King of Molorva, and I'm very happy to find you alive and well."

"And what's more, you have a grand nephew now, Uncle," King Kaffas beamed. "My Queen is here, and she was delivered of a baby boy early this morning."

9
EXPOSED SECRETS

"You escaped with the two royal crowns," the Grand Duke of Molorva chuckled and Andoria blushed deeply. "And the royal sceptre, the three emblems that the people of Molorva hold dearly. How did you do it, young lady?"

"It was the only way I could stop the coronation of those usurpers," Andoria said. "And hand them to the rightful rulers of Molorva."

"For your bravery and courage in saving and preserving the royal family of Molorva, you will be awarded one of the kingdom's highest honours," King Kaffas said. "Whatever you want, you will be given, Andoria."

But she shook her head, "Oh wise King, if you would only grant my family freedom from the bondage of servitude and slavery, that would be reward enough for me."

"Who of your family remains in Molorva?"

"My maternal uncle and cousins. My mother's family was bonded nearly two centuries ago after my ancestor caused the death of his neighbour when they were arguing over a piece of land. Our punishment was to become bonded servants and all our lands were seized so we've always been servants or slaves. Granting us our freedom to live and move freely is all I ask." She curtsied.

"And you can be sure that it will be done, and as well, your uncle will receive lands and a duchy."

"It's too much," Andoria said and to her consternation, burst into tears.

"There, there," the Grand Duke patted her lightly on the shoulder. "Your name will be spoken of in centuries to come."

Connor was so proud of the young woman who had risked her life and been so brave as to save the life of the king of her country.

The royal family and the grand duke had stayed for three more days after Christmas but were now getting ready to return home. He couldn't let Andoria go, not when he was deeply in love with her.

"Your majesty," he bowed to the king, "May I ask for something?"

"Lord Braxton, you're now an honorary citizen of Molorva and have the right to approach the king and ask for whatever it is you want. Go ahead."

"You servant humbly asks for Miss Andoria's hand in marriage."

"What?" Andoria blushed furiously, much to the delight of those present.

"She is an exceptional woman and I must admit that I fell in love with her the moment I saw her. If you would grant me her hand, I promise that she will be the most loved duchess in this kingdom."

"Andoria, what do you have to say?" The king turned his gaze on her, and she nodded because she couldn't speak. It was really happening, she was loved by a most noble man and not just because of his title, but he was also a very kind man too.

"Yes, your majesty."

"Andoria, I know I ambushed you back there, but I'm a desperate man," Connor had followed her out onto the porch to leave the king and his grand duke to discuss their kingdom matters. "But I believe you know how I feel about you."

"Isn't it too soon to fall in love?" She asked breathlessly.

"Dear beloved girl," he took her hand and led her out of sight of those in the house, "The heart wants what it wants. You see, two years ago, I was engaged to a beautiful woman but there was no love between us. It was more like an arranged marriage, but I was determined to be a good husband. Unfortunately, she was badly injured in a riding accident and was bedridden for a full year before she died. I never thought I would ever find a woman who just consumes me. My grandparents had a good marriage and they brought me up since my own parents died when I was a babe. I really wanted what they had, but since I'd never met a woman who touched my heart, I accepted to settle with Serena."

"Oh, my lord," Andoria whispered.

"Andoria, I know it's too soon but . . ."

"Yes," she nodded.

"You don't even know what I was going to ask you."

"But I'll answer you anyway because my heart is speaking to yours. I love you too, Connor, Lord Braxton of Winthrop."

"My beautiful Andoria," he kissed her gently on the lips.

10

JOURNEY'S END

"Won't you miss your home," Connor held his wife of one day close. They were seated on their favourite couch in front of the fire in the living room. "You grew up in Molorva and must have a deep attachment to the kingdom."

"But my heart was always in England, the land of my father. I longed for England, and that was why I could never accept the suit of any of the men there. Besides, as a child of a bonded family the only men allowed to offer for me were also bondmen. I wanted to be free and dreamed that I would one day come to England. That was the reason my mother ran away and come to England, so she would be free, but my father died when I was just two years old, and with no family left, she had to go back to

Molorva." She looked at him, "Papa was from Winthrop Village and his family were the Millers, do you know of them?"

Connor shook his head, "As I was growing up, my grandfather would speak of a plague that had wiped out nearly the whole village and once he mentioned a young woman from Molorva who went back to her own people."

"That was my mother."

"Most families were wiped out and those who now live here came from other parts of England. I'm really sorry."

"No, it doesn't matter because I'm home now," she lay on his chest feeling very happy. "Where you are is where my home is."

"I will forever be grateful to the Kingdom of Molorva for they were keeping and preparing you for me, my love. But we made a promise to King Kaffas and Queen Naomi that we would attend their coronation next month."

"Of course," she laughed, a delightful sound that made her husband smile. "I want to witness my beloved uncle being given the title of duke and receiving freedom for our whole lineage." She sat up, eyes glowing, "Oh Connor, I'm so happy that I feel like crying. Freedom for my people is all I ever really yearned for, and now it's going to happen."

"You're truly a remarkable and courageous woman, and I feel so blessed to be the man you have chosen as your husband, my lovely duchess."

Most of Winthrop Duchy and village had turned up for the magnificent wedding the day before, more so when they heard that the royal family of Molorva was present. And much to the villagers' delight, every household went away bearing gifts they never expected.

To the radiant bride, her journey home had come to an end. And to the happy groom, all his problems were over for before the royal family left to return to their waiting subjects just that morning, the Grand Duke presented him with a cheque that took his breath away. He could pay all his creditors and still have so much more left over to restore his duchy. It would take him time but without the debts hanging around his neck like an albatross, he was sure it would be done.

And little Silver, her majesty's gift to Andoria, lay at their feet, wagging his little tail and quite content in his new home.

EPILOGUE

Retribution against the usurper and his wife was swift, and they never saw it coming. Once the Grand Duke had established that indeed the man who had communicated with him was the true and rightful king of Molorva, he swiftly put his plans into action.

Emissaries were sent from the Duchy of Winthrop to various cities in Europe where those loyal to King Kaffas were waiting.

On New Year's Day, an army silently marched up to the palace in Longria, and without shedding a single drop of blood, took back the kingdom from the unlawful king. His trial was swift, and just as King Kaffas, his queen and the crown prince were riding into Longria in victory and being cheered on by thousands of their subjects, a well-

guarded ship left Molorva for an undisclosed destination, bearing Francis and Bernice, the usurpers.

All their friends had deserted them, and they found out the hard way that Molorvans are an unforgiving people, especially when one had betrayed their trust. No one ever heard of them again, not that anyone even cared to ask.

∽

THANK YOU FOR CHOOSING A PUREREAD BOOK!

We hope you enjoyed the story, and as a way to thank you for choosing PureRead we'd like to send you this free book, and other fun reader rewards...

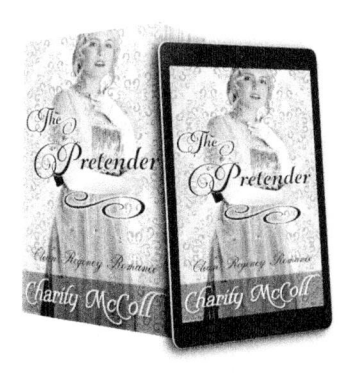

An undercover plan designed to win a young nobleman's heart is threatened when the lovely

Gabrielle Belgrade's soft conscience and honesty threatens to undo the matchmaking shenanigans of Lord Grant's well intentioned godmother.

Click here for your free copy of The Pretender
PureRead.com/regency

Thanks again for reading.
See you soon!

OUR GIFT TO YOU

AS A WAY TO SAY THANK YOU WE WOULD
LOVE TO SEND YOU THIS BEAUTIFUL
STORY FREE OF CHARGE.

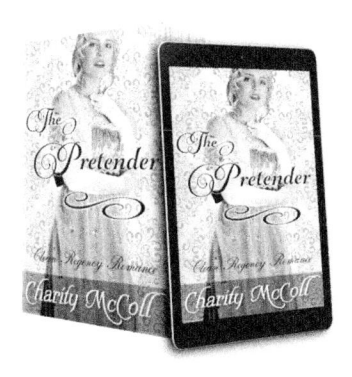

An undercover plan designed to win a young nobleman's heart is threatened when the lovely Gabrielle Belgrade's soft conscience and honesty threatens to undo the matchmaking shenanigans of Lord Grant's well intentioned godmother.

Click here for your free copy of The Pretender

PureRead.com/regency

At PureRead we publish books you can trust. Great tales without smut or swearing, but with all of the mystery and romance you expect from a great story.

Be the first to know when we release new books, take part in our fun competitions, and get surprise free books in your inbox by signing up to our free VIP Reader list.

As a thank you you'll receive a copy of **The Pretender** straight away in you inbox.

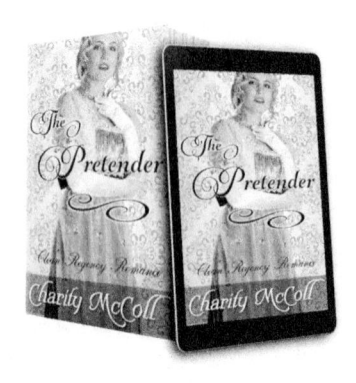

Click here for your free copy of The Pretender

PureRead.com/regency